HORRID HENRY

SUMMER OF DOOM

FRANCESCA SIMON

FRANCESCA SIMON SPENT HER CHILDHOOD ON THE BEACH IN CALIFORNIA AND STARTED WRITING STORIES AT THE AGE OF EIGHT. SHE WROTE HER FIRST HORRID HENRY BOOK IN 1994. HORRID HENRY HAS GONE ON TO CONQUER THE GLOBE; HIS ADVENTURES HAVE SOLD MILLIONS OF COPIES WORLDWIDE.

FRANCESCA HAS WON THE CHILDREN'S BOOK OF THE YEAR AWARD AND IN 2009 WAS AWARDED A GOLD BLUE PETER BADGE. SHE WAS ALSO A TRUSTEE OF THE WORLD BOOK DAY CHARITY FOR SIX YEARS.

FRANCESCA LIVES IN NORTH LONDON WITH HER FAMILY.

WWW.FRANCESCASIMON.COM WWW.HORRIDHENRY.CO.UK @SIMON_FRANCESCA

TONY ROSS

TONY ROSS WAS BORN IN LONDON AND STUDIED AT THE LIVERPOOL SCHOOL OF ART AND DESIGN. HE HAS WORKED AS A CARTOONIST, A GRAPHIC DESIGNER, AN ADVERTISING ART DIRECTOR AND A UNIVERSITY LECTURER.

TONY IS ONE OF THE MOST POPULAR AND SUCCESSFUL CHILDREN'S ILLUSTRATORS OF ALL TIME, BEST KNOWN FOR ILLUSTRATING HORRID HENRY AND THE WORKS OF DAVID WALLIAMS, AS WELL AS HIS OWN HUGELY POPULAR SERIES, THE LITTLE PRINCESS. HE LIVES IN MACCLESFIELD.

HORRID
HENRY
SUMMER OF DOOM

FRANCESCA SIMON
ILLUSTRATED BY TONY ROSS

Orion

ORION CHILDREN'S BOOKS

Stories originally published in "Horrid Henry Tricks the Tooth Fairy",
"Horrid Henry Gets Rich Quick", "Horrid Henry's Haunted House",
"Horrid Henry and the Mummy's Curse", "Horrid Henry Rocks"
and "Horrid Henry: Up, Up and Away", respectively.

This collection first published in Great Britain in 2025 by Hodder & Stoughton

1 3 5 7 9 10 8 6 4 2

A CIP catalogue record for this book is available from the British Library.

ISBN 978 1 51011 361 9

Printed and bound in Great Britain by Clays Ltd, Elcograf S.P.A.

The paper and board used in this book are from well-managed forests and
other responsible sources.

Orion Children's Books
An imprint of
Hachette Children's Group
Part of Hodder and Stoughton Limited
Carmelite House
50 Victoria Embankment
London EC4Y 0DZ

The authorised representative in the EEA is Hachette Ireland,
8 Castlecourt Centre, Dublin 15, D15 XTP3, Ireland (email: info@hbgi.ie)

An Hachette UK Company
www.hachette.co.uk

www.hachettechildrens.co.uk
www.horridhenry.co.uk

CONTENTS

MEET THE

200 CM

175 CM

150 CM

125 CM

100 CM

75 CM

50 CM

25 CM

0 CM

HENRY

PETER

HORRID HENRY'S

WEDDING

"I'm not wearing these **HORRIBLE** clothes and that's that!"

Horrid Henry glared at the mirror. A stranger smothered in a lilac ruffled shirt, green satin knickerbockers, tights, pink cummerbund tied in a *floppy bow* and pointy white satin shoes with *gold buckles* glared back at him.

Henry had never seen anyone looking so silly in his life.

"AHA HA HA HA HA!" shrieked Horrid Henry, pointing at the mirror.

Then Henry peered more closely. The ridiculous-looking boy was **HIM**.

Perfect Peter stood next to Horrid Henry. He too was smothered in a lilac ruffled shirt, green satin knickerbockers, tights, pink cummerbund tied in a *floppy bow* and pointy white satin shoes with *gold buckles*. But, unlike Henry, Peter was SMILING.

"Aren't they adorable!" squealed Prissy Polly. "That's how my children are always going to dress."

Prissy Polly was Horrid Henry's

HORRIBLE older cousin. Prissy Polly was always *squeaking* and SQUEALING:

"*Eeek*, it's a speck of dust."

"*Eeek*, it's a puddle."

"*Eeek*, my hair is a mess."

But when Prissy Polly announced she was getting married to Pimply Paul and wanted Henry and Peter to be pageboys, Mum said **YES** before Henry could stop her.

"What's a pageboy?" asked Henry suspiciously.

"A pageboy carries the wedding

rings down the aisle on a satin cushion," said Mum.

"And throws *confetti* afterwards," said Dad.

Henry liked the idea of throwing confetti. But carrying rings on a cushion? No thanks.

"**I DON'T WANT TO BE A PAGEBOY**," said Henry.

"I do, I do," said Peter.

"You're going to be a pageboy, and that's that," said Mum.

"And you'll behave yourself," said Dad. "It's very kind of Cousin Polly to ask you."

Henry **scowled**.

"Who'd want to be married to her?" said Henry. "I wouldn't if you paid me a **MILLION POUNDS**."

But for some reason the bridegroom, Pimply Paul, did want to marry Prissy Polly. And, as far as Henry knew, he had not been paid one million pounds.

Pimply Paul was also trying on his wedding clothes. He looked **ridiculous** in a black top hat, lilac shirt, and a black jacket covered in *gold swirls*.

"I won't wear these **SILLY** clothes," said Henry.

"Oh be quiet, you little **BRAT**," snapped Pimply Paul.

Horrid Henry glared at him.

"**I WON'T**," said Henry. "And that's final."

"Henry, stop being **HORRID**," said Mum. She looked extremely silly in a **BIG FLOPPY** hat dripping with flowers.

Suddenly Henry grabbed at the *lace ruffles* round his throat.

"I'm choking," he gasped.

"**I CAN'T BREATHE**."

Then Henry fell to the floor and
rolled around.

"**UGGGGGHHHHHHH**," moaned Henry.
"I'm dying."

"Get up this minute, Henry!" said
Dad.

"*Eeek*, there's dirt on the floor!"
shrieked Polly.

"Can't you control that child?" hissed Pimply Paul.

"I DON'T WANT TO BE A PAGEBOY!" howled Horrid Henry.

"Thank you so much for asking me to be a pageboy, Polly," shouted Perfect Peter, trying to be heard over Henry's screams.

"You're welcome," shouted Polly.

"**STOP THAT, HENRY!**" ordered Mum. "I've never been so ashamed in my life."

"**I HATE CHILDREN**," muttered Pimply Paul under his breath.

Horrid Henry stopped. Unfortunately, his pageboy clothes looked as *fresh* and *crisp* as ever.

All right, thought Horrid Henry. You want me at this wedding? You've got me.

Prissy Polly's wedding day arrived. Henry was delighted to see rain pouring down. How cross Polly would be.

Perfect Peter was already dressed.

"Isn't this going to be **FUN**, Henry?" said Peter.

"**NO!**" said Henry, sitting on the floor. "**AND I'M NOT GOING.**"

Mum and Dad *stuffed* Henry into his pageboy clothes. It was hard, **HEAVY** work.

Finally everyone was in the car.

"**WE'RE GOING TO BE LATE!**" shrieked Mum.

"**WE'RE GOING TO BE LATE!**" shrieked Dad.

"**WE'RE GOING TO BE LATE!**" shrieked Peter.

"Good!" muttered Henry.

Mum, Dad, Henry and Peter arrived at the church. **BOOM!** There was a *clap* of thunder. Rain poured down. All the other guests were already inside.

"Watch out for the puddle, boys," said Mum, as she leapt out of the car. She opened her umbrella.

Dad *jumped* over the puddle.

Peter *jumped* over the puddle

Herny *jumped* over the puddle, and **tripped**—

SPLASH!

"Oopsy," said Henry.

His *ruffles* were torn, his *knickerbockers* were filthy, and his satin shoes were soaked.

Mum, Dad, and Peter were covered in muddy water.

Perfect Peter **burst** into tears.

"You've ruined my pageboy clothes," sobbed Peter.

Mum wiped as much dirt as she could off Henry and Peter.

"It was an accident, Mum, really," said Henry.

"HURRY UP, YOU'RE LATE!" shouted Pimply Paul.

Mum and Dad dashed into the church. Henry and Peter stayed outside, waiting to make their entrance.

Pimply Paul and his best man,

Cross Colin, stared at Henry and Peter.

"You look a **MESS**," said Paul.

"It was an accident," said Henry.

Peter SNIVELLED.

"Now be careful with the wedding rings," said Cross Colin. He handed Henry and Peter a satin cushion each, with a gold ring on top.

A great quivering clump of lace and taffeta and bows and flowers approached. Henry guessed Prissy Polly must be lurking somewhere underneath.

"*Eeek*," squeaked the clump. "Why did it have to rain on my wedding?"

"*Eeek*," squeaked the clump again. "You're **FILTHY**."

Perfect Peter began to sob. The satin cushion trembled in his hand. The ring balanced precariously near the edge.

Cross Colin snatched Peter's cushion.

"You can't carry a ring with your hand SHAKING like that," snapped Colin. "You'd better carry them both, Henry."

"Come *on*," hissed Pimply Paul.
"We're late!"

Cross Colin and Pimply Paul
dashed into the church.

The music started. Henry pranced
down the aisle after Polly. Everyone
stood up.

Henry BEAMED and *bowed* and
waved. He was KING HENRY
THE HORRIBLE, smiling
graciously at his cheering subjects
before he **chopped** off their heads.

As he danced along, he stepped on
Polly's long, trailing dress.

RIIIIP.

"*Eeeeek!*" squeaked Prissy Polly.

Part of Polly's train lay beneath Henry's muddy satin shoe.

That dress was too long anyway, thought Henry. He KICKED the fabric out of the way and **STOMPED** down the aisle.

The bride, groom, best man and pageboys assembled in front of the minister.

Henry stood . . . and stood . . . and stood. The minister droned **on** . . . and

on . . . and **on**. Henry's arm holding up the cushion began to *ache*. This is boring, thought Henry, jiggling the rings on the cushion.

Boing! Boing! Boing!

Oooh, thought Henry. I'm good at ring tossing.

The rings **BOUNCED**.

The minister droned.

Henry was a famous pancake chef, tossing the pancakes higher and higher and higher . . .

CLINK CLUNK.

The rings rolled down the aisle and vanished down a small grate.

Oops, thought Henry.

"May I have the rings, please?" said the minister.

Everyone looked at Henry.

"He's got them," said Henry desperately, pointing at Peter.

"I have not," sobbed Peter.

Henry reached into his pocket.

He found two pieces of old **CHEWING GUM**, some *gravel* and his lucky **PIRATE** ring.

"Here, use this," he said.

At last, Pimply Paul and Prissy Polly were married.

Cross Colin handed Henry and Peter a basket of pink and yellow *rose petals* each.

"Throw the petals in front of the bride and groom as they walk back down the aisle," whispered Colin.

"I will," said Peter. He SCATTERED the petals before Pimply Paul and Prissy Polly.

"So will I," said Henry. He **HURLED** a handful of petals in Pimply Paul's face.

"Watch it, you little **BRAT**," snarled Paul.

"Windy, isn't it?" said Henry. He hurled another handful of petals at Polly.

"*Eeek*," squeaked Prissy Polly.

"Everyone outside for the photographs," said the photographer.

Horrid Henry loved having his
picture taken. He dashed out.

"Pictures of the bride and groom
first," said the photographer.

Henry **jumped** in front.

CLICK.

Henry peeked from the side.

CLICK.

Henry stuck out his tongue.

CLICK.

Henry made **HORRIBLE** rude faces.

CLICK.

"This way to the reception!" said Cross Colin.

The wedding party was held in a nearby hotel.

The adults did nothing but talk and eat, talk and drink, talk and eat.

Perfect Peter sat at the table and ate his lunch.

Horrid Henry sat under the table and poked people's legs. He crawled around and Squashed some toes. Then Henry got bored and drifted into the next room.

There was the wedding cake, standing alone, on a little table. It was the most *beautiful, delicious-looking cake* Henry had ever seen. It had three layers and was covered in **luscious** white icing and YUMMY iced flowers and bells and leaves.

Henry's mouth watered.

I'll just taste a TEENY WEENY bit of petal, thought Henry. No harm in that.

He broke off a morsel and popped it in his mouth.

HMMMM BOY! That icing tasted great.

Perhaps just one more bite, thought Henry. If I take it from the back, no one will notice.

Henry carefully selected an icing rose from the bottom tier and stuffed it in his mouth. **WOW**.

Henry stood back from the cake. It looked a little uneven now, with that rose missing from the bottom.

I'll just even it up, thought Henry. It was the work of a moment to break off a rose from the middle tier and another from the top.

Then a strange thing happened.

"**EAT ME**," whispered the cake. "**GO ON**."

Who was Henry to ignore such a request?

He **picked** out a few crumbs from the back.

Delicious, thought Henry. Then he took a few more. And a few more. Then he dug out a **NICE BIG CHUNK**.

"**WHAT DO YOU THINK YOU'RE DOING?**" shouted Pimply Paul.

Henry ran round the cake table. Paul ran after him.

Round and **_round_** and **_round_** the cake they ran.

"Just wait till I get my hands on you!" snarled Pimply Paul.

Henry dashed under the table.

Pimply Paul lunged
for him and
missed.

Pimply
Paul fell
head first on
to the cake.

SPLAT.

Henry slipped away.

Prissy Polly ran into the room.

"*Eeek*," she shrieked.

"Wasn't that a *lovely wedding*," sighed Mum on the way home. "Funny they didn't have a cake, though."

"Oh yes," said Dad.

"Oh yes," said Peter.

"OH YES!" said Henry. "I'll be glad to be a pageboy anytime."

HORRID HENRY'S

SPORTS DAY

"We all want sports day to be a great success tomorrow," announced Miss Battle-Axe. "I am here to make sure that *no one*" — she glared at Horrid Henry — "SPOILS it."

Horrid Henry glared back. Horrid Henry hated sports day. Last year he hadn't won a single event. He'd dropped his egg in the egg-and-spoon race, TRIPPED over Rude Ralph in the three-legged race, and collided with Sour Susan in the sack race. Henry's team had even lost the tug-of-war.

Most sickening of all, Perfect Peter had won *both* his races.

If only the school had a sensible day, like TV-watching day, or chocolate-eating day, or who could guzzle the most crisps day, Horrid Henry would be sure to win every prize. But no. *He* had to leap and dash about getting hot and bothered in front of stupid parents. When he became king he'd make teachers run all the races then behead the winners. KING HENRY THE HORRIBLE grinned happily.

"Pay attention, Henry!" barked Miss

Battle-Axe. "What did I just say?"

Henry had no idea. "Sports day is cancelled?" he suggested hopefully.

Miss Battle-Axe fixed him with her steely eyes. "I said no one is to bring any sweets tomorrow. You'll all be given a delicious, refreshing piece of orange."

Henry slumped in his chair, **SCOWLING**. All he could do was hope for rain.

Sports day dawned bright and sunny.

RATS, thought Henry. He could, of course, pretend to be sick. But he'd tried that last year and Mum hadn't been **FOOLED**. The year before that he'd complained he'd hurt his leg. Unfortunately Dad then caught him dancing on the table.

It was no use. He'd just have to take part. If only he could win a race!

Perfect Peter **BOUNCED** into his room.

"Sports day today!" beamed Peter. "And *I'm* responsible for bringing the hard-boiled **eggs** for the egg-and-spoon races. Isn't it exciting!"

"**NO!**" screeched Henry. "Get out of here!"

"But I only . . ." began Peter.

Henry *leapt* at him, **roaring**. He was a cowboy lassoing a runaway steer.

"**EEEAAARGH!**" SQUEALED Peter.

"Stop being **HORRID**, Henry!" 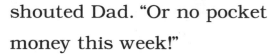 shouted Dad. "Or no pocket money this week!"

Henry let Peter go.

"It's so unfair," he muttered, picking up his clothes from the floor and putting them on. Why did he never win?

Henry reached under his bed and filled his pockets from the secret sweet tin he kept there. **Horrid Henry** was a **master** at eating sweets in school without being detected. At least he could scoff something good while the others were **STUCK** eating dried-up old orange pieces.

Then he **stomped** downstairs. Perfect Peter was busy packing hard-boiled eggs into a carton.

Horrid Henry sat down **SCOWLING** and gobbled his breakfast.

"Good luck, boys," said Mum. "I'll be there to cheer for you."

"**Humph,**" growled Henry.

"Thanks, Mum," said Peter. "I expect I'll win my egg-and-spoon race again but of course it doesn't matter if I don't. It's how you play that counts."

"**SHUT UP, PETER!**" snarled Henry. Egg-and-spoon! Egg-and-spoon!

If Henry heard that **DISGUSTING** phrase once more he would start FROTHING at the mouth.

"Mum! Henry told me to shut up," WAILED Peter, "and he **ATTACKED** me this morning."

"Stop being **HORRID**, Henry," said Mum. "Peter, come with me and we'll comb your hair. I want you to look your best when you win that trophy again."

Henry's blood boiled. He felt like *snatching* those eggs and *hurling* them against the wall.

Then Henry had a *wonderful*, **SPECTACULAR** idea. It was so wonderful that . . . Henry heard Mum coming back down the stairs. There was no time to lose crowing about his brilliance.

Horrid Henry *ran* to the fridge, grabbed another egg carton and **SWAPPED** it for the box of hard-boiled ones on the counter.

"Don't forget your eggs, Peter," said Mum. She handed the carton to Peter, who tucked it safely in his school bag.

Tee hee, thought Horrid Henry.

Henry's class lined up on the playing fields. **FLASH!** A small figure wearing gleaming white trainers *zipped* by. It was Aerobic Al, the fastest boy in Henry's class.

"Gotta run, gotta run, gotta run,"

he chanted, gliding into place beside Henry. "I will, of course, win every event," he announced. "I've been training all year. My dad's got a *special* place all ready for my trophies."

"Who wants to race anyway?" **SNEERED** Horrid Henry, sneaking a **yummy gummy fuzzball** into his mouth.

"Now, teams for the three-legged race," **BARKED** Miss Battle-Axe into her megaphone. "This is a race showing how well you co-operate and use teamwork with your partner. Ralph

55

will race with William, Josh will race with Clare, Henry . . ." she glanced at her list, ". . . you will race with Margaret."

"**NO!**" screamed Horrid Henry.

"**NO!**" screamed Moody Margaret.

"**YES**," said Miss Battle-Axe.

"But I want to be with Susan," said Margaret.

"No fussing," said Miss Battle-Axe. "Bert, where's your partner?"

"I dunno," said Beefy Bert.

Henry and Margaret stood as far apart as possible while their legs

were tied together.

"You'd better do as I say, Henry," HISSED Margaret. "*I'll* decide how we race."

"*I* will, you mean," HISSED Henry.

"**READY . . . STEADY . . . GO!**"

Miss Battle-Axe blew her whistle.

They were off! Henry moved to the left, Margaret moved to the right.

"**THIS WAY, HENRY!**" shouted Margaret. She tried to drag him.

"**No, this way!**" shouted Henry. He tried to drag her.

They *lurched* wildly, left and right, then **toppled** over.

CRASH! Aerobic Al and Lazy Linda tripped over the **SCREAMING** Henry and Margaret.

SMASH! Rude Ralph and Weepy William fell over Al and Linda.

BUMP! Dizzy Dave and Beefy Bert collided with Ralph and William.

"**WAAA!**" wailed Weepy William.

"It's all your fault, Margaret!" shouted Henry, pulling her hair.

"No, yours," shouted Margaret, pulling his harder.

Miss Battle-Axe blew her whistle frantically.

"**STOP! STOP!**" she ordered. "Henry! Margaret! What an example to set for the younger ones. Any more nonsense like that and you'll be severely punished. Everyone, get ready for the **EGG-AND-SPOON** race!"

This was it! The moment Henry

had been waiting for.

The children lined up in their teams. Moody Margaret, Sour Susan and Anxious Andrew were going first in Henry's class. Henry glanced at Peter.

Yes, there he was, smiling proudly, next to Goody-Goody Gordon, Spotless

Sam and Tidy Ted. The eggs lay still on their spoons. Horrid Henry held his breath.

"READY . . . STEADY . . . GO!" shouted Miss Battle-Axe.

They were off!

"Go, Peter, go!" shouted Mum.

Peter walked *faster* and *faster* and *faster*. He was in the lead. He was pulling away from the field. Then . . . **wobble** . . . **wobble** . . . SPLAT!

"AAAAAGH!" yelped Peter.

Moody Margaret's egg wobbled.

SPLAT!

Then Susan's.

SPLAT!

Then everybody's.

SPLAT!

SPLAT!

SPLAT!

"I've got egg on my shoes!" wailed Margaret.

"I've ruined my new dress!" **SHRIEKED** Susan.

"I've got egg all over me!" SQUEALED Tidy Ted.

"Help!" squeaked Perfect Peter. Egg dripped down his trousers.

Parents surged forward, screaming and waving handkerchiefs and towels.

Rude Ralph and Horrid Henry **SHRIEKED** with laughter.

Miss Battle-Axe blew her whistle.

"Who brought the **eggs?**" asked Miss Battle-Axe. Her voice was like ice.

"I did," said Perfect Peter. "But I brought hard-boiled ones."

"**OUT!**" shouted Miss Battle-Axe.

"Out of the games!"

"But . . . but . . ." gasped Perfect Peter.

"No buts, out!" She glared. "Go straight to the Head."

Perfect Peter **burst** into tears and crept away.

Horrid Henry could hardly contain himself. This was the **BEST** sports day he'd ever been to.

"The rest of you, stop laughing at once. Parents, get back to your seats! Time for the next race!" ordered Miss Battle-Axe.

All things considered, thought **Horrid Henry**, lining up with his class, it hadn't been too TERRIBLE a day. He'd loved the egg-and-spoon race, of course. And he'd had FUN *pulling* the other team into a muddy puddle in the tug-of-war, knocking over the obstacles in the obstacle race, and **crashing** into Aerobic Al in the sack race.

But, oh, to actually win something!

There was just one race left before sports day was over. The cross-country run. The event Henry **HATED** more than any other. One long, sweaty, **EXHAUSTING** lap round the whole field.

Henry heaved his heavy bones to the starting line. His final chance to win . . . yet he knew there was no hope. If he beat Weepy William he'd be doing well.

Suddenly Henry had a *wonderful*, **SPECTACULAR IDEA**. Why

had he never thought of this before? Truly, he was a genius. Wasn't there some ancient Greek who'd won a race by throwing down golden apples which his rival kept stopping to pick up? Couldn't he, Henry, learn something from those old Greeks?

"**READY**...**STEADY**...**GO!**" shrieked Miss Battle-Axe.

Off they *dashed*.

"Go, Al, go!" yelled his father.

"Get a move on, Margaret!" **SHRIEKED** her mother.

"Go, Ralph!" cheered his father.

"Do your best, Henry," said Mum.

Horrid Henry reached into his pocket and hurled some sweets. They **THUDDED** to the ground in front of the runners.

"Look, sweets!" shouted Henry.

Al checked behind him. He was well in the lead. He paused and scooped up one sweet, and then another. He glanced behind again, then started unwrapping the **yummy gummy fuzzball**.

"Sweets!" yelped Greedy Graham. He stopped to pick up as many as he

could find then stuffed them in his
mouth.

"*YUMMY!*" screamed Graham.

"*Sweets!* Where?" chanted the
others. Then they stopped to look.

"Over there!" yelled Henry, throwing
another handful. The racers paused
to *pounce* on the treats.

While the others **MUNCHED** and **CRUNCHED**, Henry made a frantic dash for the lead.

He was out in front! Henry's legs moved as they had never moved before, pounding round the field. And there was the finishing line!

THUD! THUD! THUD!

Henry glanced back. Oh no! Aerobic Al was catching up!

Henry felt in his pocket. He had one **GIANT** gob-stopper left. He looked round, panting.

"Go home and take a nap, Henry!"

shouted Al, sticking out his tongue as he raced past.

Henry threw down the gob-stopper in front of Al. Aerobic Al hesitated, then *skidded* to a halt and picked it up. He could beat Henry any day so why not show off a bit?

Suddenly Henry *sprinted* past. Aerobic Al dashed after him. **Harder** and **harder**, *faster* and *faster* Henry ran. He was a bird. He was a plane. He flew across the finishing line.

"The winner is . . . Henry?" squeaked Miss Battle-Axe.

71

"I'VE BEEN ROBBED!"

screamed Aerobic Al.

"HURRAY!" yelled Henry.

Wow, what a great day, thought

Horrid Henry, proudly carrying home

his trophy. Al's dad shouting at Miss
Battle-Axe and Mum. Miss Battle-Axe
and Mum shouting back. Peter sent
off in DISGRACE. And he, Henry,
the big winner.

"I can't think how you got those
eggs muddled up," said Mum.

"Me neither," said Perfect Peter,
SNIFFLING.

"Never mind, Peter," said
Henry brightly. "It's not
winning, it's *how you play
that counts*."

HORRID HENRY'S

SCHOOL FAIR

"Henry! Peter! I need your donations to the school fair NOW!"

Mum was in a bad mood. She was helping MOODY MARGARET'S mum organise the fair and had been nagging Henry for ages to give away some of his old games and toys. Horrid Henry hated giving. He liked getting.

Horrid Henry stood in his bedroom. Everything he owned was on the floor.

"How about giving away those bricks?" said Mum. "You never play with them any more."

"**NO!**" said Henry. They were bound to come in useful some day.

"How about some soft toys? When was the last time you played with Spotty Dog?"

"**NO!**" said Horrid Henry. "He's mine!"

Perfect Peter appeared in the doorway dragging two enormous sacks.

"Here's my contribution to the school fair, Mum," said Perfect Peter.

Mum peeped inside the bags.

"Are you sure you want to give away so many toys?" said Mum.

"Yes," said Peter. "I'd like other children to have fun playing with them."

"What a generous boy you are, Peter," Mum said, giving him a BIG HUG.

Henry **SCOWLED**. Peter could give away all his toys, for all Henry cared. Henry wanted to keep everything.

Wait! How could he have forgotten?

Henry reached under his bed and pulled out a large box hidden under a blanket. The box contained all the *useless*, **horrible** presents Henry had ever received. Packs of hankies. Vests with ducks on them. A nature guide. UGGH! HENRY HATED NATURE. Why would anyone want to waste their time looking at pictures of flowers and trees?

And then, right at the bottom, was the worst present of all. A Walkie-Talkie-

Burpy-Slurpy-Teasy-Weasy Doll. He'd got it for Christmas from a great-aunt he'd never met. The card she'd written was still attached.

Dear Henrietta

I thought this doll would be perfect for a sweet little two-year-old like you! Take good care of your new baby!

Love

Great-Aunt Greta

Even worse, she'd sent Peter
something brilliant.

Dear Pete

*You must be a teenager by now and too old for
toys, so here's £25. Don't spend it all on sweets!*

Love

Great-Aunt Greta

Henry had **SCREAMED** and **begged**,
but Peter got to keep the money, and
Henry was stuck with
the doll. He was far
too embarrassed to

try to sell it, so the doll just lived
hidden under his bed with all the
other **rotten** gifts.

"Take that," said Henry, giving the
doll a kick.

"Mama Mama Mama!" burbled the
doll. "Baby burp!"

"Not Great-Aunt Greta's present!"
said Mum.

"Take it or leave it," said Henry.
"You can have the rest as well."

Mum sighed. "Some LUCKY children
are going to be very happy." She took
the hateful presents and put them in

the jumble sack.

Phew! He'd got rid of that doll at last! He'd lived in **TERROR** of Rude Ralph or **MOODY MARGARET** coming over and finding it. Now he'd never have to see that **burping slurping** long-haired thing again.

Henry crept into the spare room where Mum was keeping all the donated toys and games for the fair. He thought he'd have a quick poke around and see what **GOOD STUFF**

would be for sale tomorrow. That way he could make a *dash* and be first in the queue.

There were rolls of raffle tickets, bottles of wine, the barrel for the lucky dip, and sacks and sacks of toys. **WOW, WHAT A HOARD!** Henry just had to move that rolled-up poster out of the way and start rummaging!

Henry pushed aside the poster and then stopped.

I wonder what this is, he thought. I think I'll just unroll it and have a little peek. No harm in that.

Carefully, he untied the ribbon and laid the poster flat on the floor. Then he gasped.

This wasn't jumble. It was the **TREASURE MAP**! Whoever guessed where the treasure was hidden always won a *fabulous prize*. Last year Sour Susan had won a **SKATEBOARD**. The year before Jolly Josh had won a **Super Soaker 2000**. Boy, it sure was worth trying to find that treasure! Horrid Henry usually had at least five goes. But his luck was so bad he had never even come close.

Henry looked at the map. There
was the island, with its caves and
lagoons, and the sea surrounding
it, filled with **WHALES** and **SHARKS** and
PIRATE SHIPS. The map was divided
into a hundred numbered squares.

Somewhere under one of those squares was an **X**.

I'll just admire the lovely picture, thought Henry. He stared and stared.

No **X**. He ran his hands over the map. No **X**.

Henry sighed. It was so unfair!

He never won anything. And this year the prize was sure to be a **Super Soaker 5000**.

Henry lifted the map to roll it up.

As he raised the thick paper to the light, a large, unmistakable **X** was suddenly visible beneath square 42.

The treasure was just under the whale's eye.

He had discovered the secret.

"**YES!**" said Horrid Henry, punching the air. "It's my lucky day, at last!"

But wait. Mum was in charge of the Treasure Map stall. If he was first in the queue and instantly bagged square 42 she was sure to be suspicious. So how could he let a few other children go first, but make sure none of them chose the right square? And then suddenly, he had a brilliant, **SPECTACULAR** idea . . .

"Tra la la la la!" trilled Horrid Henry,
as he, Peter, Mum and Dad walked to
the school fair.

"You're cheerful today, Henry," said
Dad.

"I'm feeling lucky," said **Horrid Henry**.

He burst into the playground and
went straight to the **TREASURE MAP** stall.

A large queue of eager children

keen to pay 20p for a chance to
guess had already formed. There was
the mystery prize, a large, tempting,
Super Soaker-sized box. **WHEEEE!**

Rude Ralph was first in line.

"PSST, RALPH," whispered Henry. "I know
where X marks the spot. I'll tell you
if you give me 50p."

"Deal," said Ralph.

"92," whispered Henry.

"Thanks!" said Ralph. He wrote his
name in square 92 and walked off,
whistling.

Moody Margaret was next.

"PSSST, MARGARET," whispered Henry.

"I know where **X** marks the spot."

"Where?" said Margaret.

"Pay me 50p and I'll tell you," whispered Henry.

"Why should I trust you?" said Margaret loudly.

Henry shrugged.

"Don't trust me then, and I'll tell Susan," said Henry.

Margaret gave Henry 50p.

"2," whispered **Horrid Henry**.

Margaret wrote her name in square 2, and skipped off.

Henry told Lazy Linda the treasure square was 4.

Henry told Dizzy Dave the treasure square was 100.

Weepy William was told 22.

Anxious Andrew was told 14.

Then Henry thought it was time he bagged the winning square. He made sure none of the children he'd tricked were nearby, then *pushed* into the queue behind Beefy Bert. His pockets BULGED with cash.

"What number do you want, Bert?" asked Henry's mum.

"I dunno," said Bert.

"Hi, Mum," said Henry. "Here's my 20p. Hmmm, now where could that treasure be?"

Horrid Henry pretended to study the map.

"I think I'll try 37," he said. "No, wait, 84. Wait, wait, I'm still deciding ..."

"Hurry up, Henry," said Mum. "Other children want to have a go."

"Okay, 42," said Henry.

Mum looked at him. Henry smiled at her and wrote his name in the square.

Then he *sauntered* off.

He could feel that **Super Soaker** in his hands already. Wouldn't it be fun to spray the teachers!

Horrid Henry had a fabulous day. He
threw wet sponges at Miss Battle-
Axe in the "BIFF A TEACHER" stall.
He joined in his class square dance.
He got a marble in the lucky dip.
Henry didn't even SCREAM when
Perfect Peter won a box of notelets
in the raffle and Henry didn't win
anything, despite spending £3 on
tickets.

**"TIME TO FIND THE WINNER OF
THE TREASURE MAP COMPETITION,"**
boomed a voice over the playground.
Everyone stampeded to the stall.

Suddenly Henry had a **terrible** thought. What if Mum had switched the **X** to a different spot at the last minute? He couldn't bear it. He absolutely couldn't bear it. He had to have that **Super Soaker!**

"And the winning number is . . ."

Mum lifted up the Treasure Map . . .

"42! The winner is — Henry."

"**YES!**" screamed Henry.

"**WHAT?**" screamed Rude Ralph, Moody Margaret, Lazy Linda, Weepy William and Anxious Andrew.

"Here's your prize, Henry," said Mum.

She handed Henry the ENORMOUS box.

"Congratulations." She did not look very pleased.

Eagerly, Henry tore off the wrapping paper. His prize was a Walkie-Talkie-Burpy-Slurpy-Teasy-Weasy Doll.

"Mama Mama Mama!" burbled the doll. "Baby slurp!"

"AAARRGGGHHHH!" howled Henry.

HORRID
HENRY'S

SWIMMING
LESSON

Oh no! thought Horrid Henry. He pulled the duvet tightly over his head.

It was Thursday. **HORRIBLE, HORRIBLE THURSDAY**. The worst day of the week. Horrid Henry was certain Thursdays came more often than any other day.

Thursday was his class *swimming* day. Henry had a nagging feeling that this Thursday was even **WORSE** than all the other **AWFUL** Thursdays.

Thursday
June 22

Horrid Henry liked the bus
ride to the pool. Horrid Henry liked
doing the dance of the seven towels
in the changing room. He also liked
HIDING in the lockers, *throwing*
socks in the pool and **splashing**
everyone.

The only thing Henry didn't like about **GOING** swimming was . . .

SWIMMING.

The truth was, Horrid Henry hated water. **UGGGH!** Water was so . . . **wet!** And *soggy*. The chlorine *stung* his eyes. He never knew what **horrors** might be lurking in the deep end. And the pool was so **cold** penguins could fly in for the winter.

Fortunately, Henry had a *brilliant* list of excuses. He'd pretend he had a **verruca**, or a **tummy ache**, or had lost his swimming costume.

Unfortunately, the **MEAN**, **NASTY**,

HORRIBLE swimming teacher, Soggy Sid, usually made him get in the pool anyway.

Then Henry would **DUCK** Dizzy Dave, or **splash** Weepy William, or **PINCH** Gorgeous Gurinder, until Sid ordered him out. It was not surprising that Horrid Henry had never managed to get his five-metre badge.

ARRRGH! Now he remembered. Today was test day. The **terrible** day when everyone had to show how far they could swim. Aerobic Al was going for gold. Moody Margaret was going for SILVER. The only ones who were still trying for their five-metre badges were Lazy Linda and Horrid Henry. **FIVE WHOLE METRES!** How could anyone swim such a vast distance?

If only they were tested on who could SINK to the bottom of the pool the fastest, or **splash** the most, or spit water the furthest, then Horrid Henry would have every badge in a jiffy. But no. He had to leap into a **FREEZING COLD POOL**, and, if he survived that shock, somehow thrash his way across five whole metres without drowning.

Well, there was **NO WAY** he was going to school today.

Mum came into his room.

"I can't go to school today, Mum," Henry moaned. "I feel **terrible**."

Mum didn't even look at him.

"**THURSDAY-ITIS** again, I presume," said Mum.

"No way!" said Henry. "I didn't even know it was Thursday."

"Get up, Henry," said Mum. "You're going swimming and that's that."

Perfect Peter peeked round the door.

"It's badge day today!" he said. "I'm going for fifty metres!"

"That's **brilliant**, Peter," said Mum. "I bet you're the best swimmer in your class."

Perfect Peter smiled modestly.

"I just try my best," he said. "Good luck with your five-metre badge, Henry," he added.

Horrid Henry **GROWLED** and **attacked**. He was a **VENUS FLYTRAP** slowly mashing a frantic fly between his deadly leaves.

"Eeeeeowwww!" screeched Peter.
"Stop being **horrid**, Henry!"
screamed Mum. "Leave your poor
brother alone!"

Horrid Henry let Peter go. If
only he could find some way not to

take his swimming test he'd be the happiest boy in the world.

Henry's class arrived at the pool. Right, thought Henry. Time to unpack his excuses to Soggy Sid.

"I can't go swimming, I've got a **verruca**," lied Henry.

"**TAKE OFF YOUR SOCK**," ordered Soggy Sid.

RATS, thought Henry.

"Maybe it's better now," said Henry.

"I thought so," said Sid.

Horrid Henry grabbed his stomach.

"**Tummy pains!**" he moaned. "I feel terrible."

"You seemed fine when you were prancing round the pool a moment ago," snapped Sid. "**NOW GET CHANGED.**"

Time for the **KILLER EXCUSE**.

"I forgot my swimming costume!" said Henry. This was his best chance of success.

"No problem," said Soggy Sid. He handed Henry a bag. "Put on one of these."

SLOWLY, Horrid Henry rummaged in

the bag. He pulled out a bikini top, a blue costume with a **HOLE** in the middle, a pair of pink pants, a TINY pair of green trunks, a polka-dot one-piece with bunnies, see-through white shorts, and a nappy.

"**I can't wear any of these!**" protested Horrid Henry.

"YOU CAN AND YOU WILL, IF I HAVE TO PUT THEM ON YOU MYSELF," snarled Sid.

Horrid Henry SQUEEZED into the green trunks. He could barely breathe. Slowly, he joined the rest of his class *pushing* and **shoving** by the side of the pool.

Everyone had **MILLIONS** of badges sewn all over their costumes. You couldn't even see Aerobic Al's bathing suit beneath the stack of badges.

"HEY YOU!" shouted Soggy

Sid. He pointed at Weepy William.

"Where's your swimming costume?"

Weepy William glanced down and **burst** into tears.

"WAAAAAH," he wailed, and ran weeping back to the changing room.

"**NOW GET IN!**" ordered Soggy Sid.

"**BUT I'LL DROWN!**" screamed Henry. "**I CAN'T SWIM!**"

"**GET IN!**" screamed Soggy Sid.

Goodbye, cruel world. Horrid Henry held his breath and fell into the icy water. **ARRRRGH!** He was turning into an iceberg!

He was **DYING!** He was **DEAD!** His feet flailed madly as he sank

DOWN,
DOWN,
DOWN
– clunk!

Henry's feet touched the bottom.

Henry stood up, **CHOKING** and **spluttering**. He was waist-deep in water.

"LINDA AND HENRY! SWIM FIVE METRES – NOW!"

What am I going to do? thought Henry. It was so humiliating not even being able to swim five metres! Everyone would TEASE him. And he'd have to listen to them **bragging** about their badges! Wouldn't it be great to get a badge? Somehow?

Lazy Linda set off, VERY VERY SLOWLY. Horrid Henry grabbed on to her leg. Maybe she'll pull me across, he thought.

"UGGGH!" gurgled Lazy Linda.

"LEAVE HER ALONE!" shouted Sid.

"LAST CHANCE, HENRY."

Horrid Henry ran along the pool's bottom and *flapped* his arms, pretending to swim.

"Did it!" said Henry.

Soggy Sid scowled.

"I SAID SWIM, NOT WALK!" screamed Sid. "You've failed. Now

get over to the far lane and practise. Remember, anyone who stops swimming during the test doesn't get a badge."

Horrid Henry **Stomped** over to the far lane. No way was he going to practise! **HOW HE HATED SWIMMING!** He watched the others splashing UP and DOWN, UP and DOWN. There was Aerobic Al, doing his laps like a bolt of lightning. And MOODY MARGARET. And Kung-Fu Kate. Everyone would be getting a badge but Henry. It was so unfair.

"PSSST, SUSAN," said Henry. "Have you

heard? There's a **SHARK** in the
deep end!"

"Oh yeah, right," said Sour Susan.
She looked at the **DARK** water in the
far end of the pool.

"Don't believe me," said Henry.
"Find out the hard way. Come back
with a leg missing."

Sour Susan paused and WHISPERED

something to Moody Margaret.

"**SHUT UP, HENRY**," said Margaret.
They swam off.

"Don't worry about the shark,
Andrew," said Henry. "I think he's
already eaten today."

"**WHAT SHARK?**" said Anxious
Andrew.

Andrew stared at the deep end. It did look awfully dark down there.

"Start swimming, Andrew!" shouted Soggy Sid.

"I don't want to," said Andrew.

"Swim! Or I'll BITE you myself!" snarled Sid.

Andrew started swimming.

"Dave, Ralph, Clare and Bert – start swimming!" bellowed Soggy Sid.

"Look out for the **SHARK!**" said Horrid Henry. He watched Aerobic Al tearing up and down the lane.

"GOTTA SWIM, GOTTA SWIM, GOTTA SWIM,"

muttered Al between strokes.

What a show-off, thought Henry. Wouldn't it be fun to play a **TRICK** on him?

Horrid Henry pretended he was a **CROCODILE**. He sneaked under the water to the middle of the pool and waited until Aerobic Al swam overhead. Then Horrid Henry reached up.

PINCH! Henry grabbed Al's thrashing leg.

"**AAAARGGGH!**" screamed Al. "Something's grabbed my leg. Help!"

Aerobic Al leapt out of the pool.

Tee hee, thought Horrid Henry.

"**IT'S A SHARK!**" screamed Sour Susan. She scrambled out of the pool.

"**THERE'S A SHARK IN THE POOL!**" screeched Anxious Andrew.

"**There's a shark in the pool!**"

howled Rude Ralph.

Everyone was screaming and shouting and struggling to get out.

The only one left in the pool was Henry.

shark!

Horrid Henry forgot there were no sharks in swimming pools.

Horrid Henry forgot *he'd* started the shark rumour.

Horrid Henry forgot he couldn't swim.

All he knew was that he was alone
in the pool – **WITH A SHARK!**
Horrid Henry swam for his life.
SHAKING and QUAKING, **splashing** and

crashing, he torpedoed his way to the side of the pool and scrambled out. He gasped and panted. Thank goodness. Safe at last! He'd never ever go swimming again.

"**FIVE METRES!**" bellowed Soggy Sid. "You've all failed your badges today, except for — Henry!"

"**WAAAAAAAHHHHHH!**" wailed the other children.

"**Whoopee!**" **screamed Henry. "Olympics, here I come!**"

HORRID
HENRY
ROCK STAR

"Boys, I have a very special treat for you," said Mum, beaming.

Horrid Henry looked up from his Mutant Max comic.

Perfect Peter looked up from his spelling homework.

A treat? A **special** treat? A VERY SPECIAL treat? Maybe Mum and Dad were finally appreciating him. Maybe they'd got tickets . . . maybe they'd actually got tickets . . . **Horrid Henry's** heart leapt. Could it be possible that at last, at long last, he'd get to go to a **Killer Boy Rats** concert?

"We're going to the **Daffy and her Dancing Daisies** show!" said Mum. "I got the last four tickets."

"OOOOOOHHHH," said Peter, clapping his hands. "**YIPPEE!** I love Daffy."

what?? NOOOOOOOOOO! That wasn't a treat. That was **TORTURE**. A treat would be a day at the **FROSTY FREEZE ICE CREAM FACTORY**. A treat would be no school. A treat would be all he could eat at **Gobble and Go**.

"I don't want to see that stupid Daffy," said Horrid Henry. "I want to see the **Killer Boy Rats**."

"No way," said Mum.

"I don't like the **Killer Boy Rats**," shuddered Peter. "Too scary."

"Me neither," shuddered Mum. "Too loud."

"Me neither," shuddered Dad. "Too **SHOUTY**."

"**NOOOOOOOO!**" screamed Henry.

"But Henry," said Peter, "everyone loves Daffy."

"Not me," snarled Henry.

133

Daffy sings and dances her way across the stage and into your heart. Your chance to sing along to all your favourite daisy songs! I'm a Lazy Daisy. Whoops-a-Daisy. And of course, Upsy-Daisy, Crazy Daisy, Prance and Dance-a-Daisy.
With special guest star Busy Lizzie!!!

Perfect Peter waved a leaflet. "Daffy's going to be the **GREATEST SHOW EVER**. Read this."

AAAAARRRRRGGGGGHHHHHH.

Moody Margaret's parents were taking her to the **Killer Boy Rats** concert. Rude Ralph was going to

the **Killer Boy Rats**
concert. Even Anxious
Andrew was going,
and he didn't even like
them. **STUCK-UP STEVE** had
been bragging for months that he
was going and would be sitting in a
special box. It was so unfair.

No one was a bigger **Rats** fan than
Horrid Henry. Henry had all their
albums: *Killer Boy Rats Attack-Tack-Tack*, *Killer Boy Rats Splat!* and
Killer Boy Rats Manic Panic.

"**IT'S NOT FAIR!**" screamed Horrid Henry. "I want to see the Killers!!!!"

"We have to see something that everyone in the family will like," said Mum. "Peter's too young for the **Killer Boy Rats** but we can all enjoy Daffy."

"Not me!" screamed Henry.

Oh, why did he have such a stupid nappy baby for a brother? Younger brothers should be banned. They just wrecked everything. When he was **KING HENRY THE HORRIBLE**, all younger brothers would be

arrested and dumped in a volcano.

In fact, why wait?

Horrid Henry pounced. He was a fiery god scooping up a human sacrifice and hurling him into the volcano's molten depths.

"AAAIIIIIEEEEEEE!" screamed Perfect Peter. "Henry attacked me."

"Stop being **HORRID**, Henry!" shouted Mum. "Leave your brother alone."

"I won't go to Daffy," yelled Henry. "And you can't make me."

"Go to your room," said Dad.

Horrid Henry paced up and down his bedroom, singing his favourite Rats song at the top of his lungs:

"I'M DEAD, YOU'RE DEAD, WE'RE DEAD. GET OVER IT.
DEAD IS GREAT, DEAD'S WHERE IT'S AT 'CAUSE . . ."

"Henry! Be quiet!" screamed Dad.

"I am being quiet!" bellowed Henry.

Honestly. Now, how could he get out of going to that terrible Daffy concert? He'd easily be the oldest one there. Only STUPID babies liked Daffy. If the **horrible** songs didn't kill him then he was sure to die of embarrassment. Then they'd be sorry they'd made him go. But it would be too late. Mum and Dad and Peter could sob and **boo hoo** all they liked but he'd still be dead. And serve them right for being so mean to him.

Dad said if he was good he could see the Killer Boys next time they

were in town. Ha. The **Killer Boy Rats**
NEVER gave concerts. Next time they
did he'd be old and hobbling and
whacking Peter with his cane.

He had to get a **Killer Boys** ticket
now. He just had to. But how? They'd
been sold out for weeks.

Maybe he could place an ad:

> CAN YOU HELP?
> DESERVING BOY SUFFERING FROM RARE AND TERRIBLE
> ILLNESS. HIS EARS ARE FALLING OFF. DOCTOR HAS PRESCRIBED
> THE KILLER BOY RATS CURE. ONLY BY HEARING THE RATS
> LIVE IS THERE ANY HOPE. IF YOU'VE GOT A TICKET TO THE
> CONCERT ON SATURDAY PLEASE SEND IT TO HENRY NOW.
> (IF YOU DON'T YOU KNOW YOU'LL BE SORRY.)

That might work. Or he could tell people that the concert was **CURSED** and anyone who went would turn into a rat. Hmmm. Somehow Henry didn't see Margaret falling for that. Too bad Peter didn't have a ticket, thought Henry sadly, he could tell him he'd turn into a killer and Peter would hand over the ticket instantly.

And then suddenly **Horrid Henry** had a *brilliant*, **SPECTACULAR** idea. There must be someone out there who was desperate for a Daffy ticket. In fact there must be someone out there who would swap a Killers ticket for a Daffy one. It was certainly worth a try.

"Hey, Brian, I hear you've got a **Killer Boy Rats** ticket," said Horrid Henry at school the next day.

"So?" said Brainy Brian.

"I've got a ticket to something much better," said Henry.

"What?" said Brian. "The Killers are the best."

Horrid Henry could barely force the grisly words out of his mouth. He twisted his lips into a smile.

"Daffy and her Dancing Daisies," said Horrid Henry.

Brainy Brian stared at him.

"Daffy and her Dancing Daisies?" he spluttered.

"Yes," said Horrid Henry brightly. "I've heard it's their BEST SHOW

143

EVER. Great new songs. You'd love it. Wanna swap?"

Brainy Brian stared at him as if he had a **TURNIP** instead of a head.

"You're trying to swap *Daffy and her Dancing Daisies* tickets for the **Killer Boy Rats?**" said Brian slowly.

"I'm doing you a favour, no one likes the Killer Boy Rats any more," said Henry.

"I do," said Brian.

RATS.

"How come you have a ticket for Daffy?" said Brian. "Isn't that a baby show?"

"It's not mine, I found it," said Horrid Henry quickly. **OOpS**.

"Ha ha, Henry, I'm seeing the Killers, and you're not," Margaret taunted.

"Yeah, Henry," said Sour Susan.

"I heard . . ." Margaret doubled over laughing, "I heard you were going to the Daffy show!"

"That's a **big fat lie**," said Henry

hotly. "I wouldn't be seen **DEAD** there."

Horrid Henry looked around the auditorium at the sea of little baby nappy faces. There was Needy Neil, clutching his mother's hand. There was Weepy William, crying because he'd **dropped** his ice cream. There was Toddler Tom, up past his bedtime. Oh, no! There was Lisping Lily. Henry ducked.

Phew. She hadn't seen him.

Margaret would never stop teasing him if she ever found out. When he was *king*, Daffy and her Dancing Daisies would live in a **dungeon** with only **RATS** for company. Anyone who so much as mentioned the name Daffy, or even grew a daisy, would be flushed down the toilet.

There was a round of polite applause as Daffy and her Dancing Daisies pirouetted on stage. **Horrid Henry** slumped in his seat as far as he could slump and pulled his cap over his face. Thank goodness he'd come disguised and brought some earplugs. No one would ever know he'd been.

"**TRA LA LA LA LA LA LA!**" trilled the Daisies.

"**TRA LA LA LA LA LA LA!**" trilled the audience.

Oh, the torture, groaned **Horrid Henry** as **HORRIBLE** song followed horrible song. Perfect Peter sang along. So did Mum and Dad.

AAARRRRRGGGHHHHH.
And to think that tomorrow
night the **Killer Boy Rats** would be
performing . . . and he wouldn't be
there! It was so unfair.

Then Daffy cartwheeled to the
front of the stage. One of the daisies
stood beside her holding a giant hat.

"And now the moment all you
Daffy Daisy fans have been waiting
for," squealed Daffy. "It's the **Lucky
Ducky Daisy Draw**, when we call up
on stage an oh-so-lucky audience
member to lead us in the **Whoops-a-**

Daisy sing-along song! Who's it going to be?"

"Me!" squealed Peter. Mum squeezed his arm.

Daffy fumbled in the hat and pulled out a ticket.

"And the lucky winner of our ticket raffle is . . . **HENRY!** Ticket 597!

Ticket 597, yes Henry, you in row P, seat 10, come on up! Daffy needs you on stage!"

Horrid Henry was stuck to his seat in horror. It must be some other Henry. Never in his **WORST NIGHTMARES** had he ever imagined—

"Henry, that's you," said Perfect Peter. "You're so lucky."

"HENRY! COME ON UP, HENRY!" shrieked Daffy. "Don't be shy!"

On stage at the Daffy show? No! No! Wait till **MOODY MARGARET** found

out. Wait till anyone found out. Henry
would never hear the end of it. He
wasn't moving. Pigs would fly before
he budged.

"Henwy!" squealed Lisping Lily
behind him. "Henwy! I want to give
you a big kiss, Henwy . . ."

Horrid Henry leapt out of his
seat. Lily! Lisping Lily! That fiend
in toddler's clothing would stop at
nothing to get hold of him. Before

Henry knew what had happened, ushers dressed as daisies had nabbed him and pushed him on stage.

Horrid Henry blinked in the lights. Was anyone in the world as unlucky as he?

"All together now, everyone get ready to ruffle their petals. Let's sing *Tippy-toe daisy do / Let us sing a song for you!*" beamed Daffy. "Henry, you start us off."

Horrid Henry stared at the vast audience. Everyone was looking at him. Of course he didn't know any

153

STUPID Daisy songs. He always blocked his ears or ran from the room whenever Peter sang them. Whatever could the words be . . .

"Watch out, whoop-di-do

Daisy's doing a big poo?"

These poor stupid kids. If only they could hear some decent songs, like . . . like . . .

"GRANNY ON HER CRUTCHES
PUSH HER OFF HER CHAIR
SHOVE SHOVE SHOVE SHOVE
SHOVE HER DOWN THE STAIRS!"

shrieked Horrid Henry.

The audience was silent. Daffy looked stunned.

"Uh, Henry . . . that's not Tippy-toe daisy do," whispered Daffy.

"C'mon everyone, join in with me," shouted Horrid Henry, spinning round and twirling in his best

Killer Boy Rats manner.

"I'M IN MY COFFIN
NO TIME FOR COUGHIN'
WHEN YOU'RE SQUISHED DOWN DEAD.
DON'T CARE IF YOU'RE A BOFFIN
DON'T CARE IF YOU'RE A LOONY,
DON'T CARE IF YOU'RE CARTOONY
I'LL SQUISH YOU!"

sang Horrid Henry as loud as he could.

"GONNA BE A ROCK STAR (AND YOU AIN'T)
DON'T EVEN–"

Two security guards ran on stage and grabbed **Horrid Henry**.

"Killer Boy Rats for ever!" shrieked Henry, as he was dragged off.

Horrid Henry *stared* at the special delivery letter covered in skulls and crossbones. His hand shook.

HEY HENRY,
WE SAW A VIDEO OF YOU SINGING OUR SONGS AND GETTING YANKED OFF STAGE – WAY TO GO, KILLER BOY! HERE'S A PAIR OF TICKETS FOR OUR CONCERT TONIGHT, AND A BACKSTAGE PASS – SEE YOU THERE.
        THE KILLER BOY RATS

Horrid Henry goggled at the tickets and the backstage pass. He couldn't move. He couldn't breathe. He was going to the **Killer Boy Rats** concert. He was actually going to the **Killer Boy Rats** concert.

Life, thought Horrid Henry, beaming, was sweet.

HORRID HENRY
AND THE ZOOM OF DOOM

BOB BOB **BOB** BOB **BOB.**

The giant teacups bobbed down the lazy river.

"*Wheeeeeeee*," squealed Perfect Peter.

"*Wheeeeeeee*," squealed Tidy Ted.

"*Wheeeeeeee*," squealed Perky Parveen.

"*Wheeeeeee!*" squealed all the mini ninnies seated in the giant floating teacups.

~~TERRIFIED SCREAMS~~ rang out from a nearby ride. Moody Margaret and Sour Susan and Brainy Brian and Jazzy Jim were *whizzing* down **Belly Flop Drop** in a **bouncing** rubber raft which twisted and looped and spun backwards.

"**DUCK**," hissed Henry. "Don't let them see us."

Horrid Henry and RUDE RALPH slunk down in their little seats as low as they could. If Margaret or any of their classmates saw them riding in the *toddler teacups*, their names would

be **MUD** for ever.

"Sit up, Henry," said Miss Battle-Axe. "You too, Ralph."

Horrid Henry groaned.

How had he, Horrid Henry, ended up trapped in a giant teacup with **MISS BATTLE-AXE** and his *wormy worm* brother and the rest of *Miss Lovely's* infant class at **WILD WATER-SLIDE PARK**? He wanted to go racing down the **ZOOM OF DOOM**, the *TWISTING*, *LOOPING*, rollercoaster waterslide with the world's **STEEPEST** drop. Where cannonballs blasted you as you hurtled backwards through waterfalls, flipping you upside down and spinning you as you crashed **SCREAMING** into Crocodile Creek. Or **Belly Flop Drop**, with its jet sprays and stomach-churning twists. Or **CRASH SPLASH**, where rubber rings raced towards each other before veering off into **TUNNELS OF TERROR**.

The shame. The misery. The horror of being trapped in giant *teacups* instead. With — oh **WOE** — only more *baby* rides to come.

It was so unfair. He'd worked his **fingers** to the **bone** earning all those badges.

Was it his fault he'd disappeared with **RUDE RALPH** on the last class trip? The class had got lost, not them. Or that he'd jumped from the little white train **chugging** around the Second World War airfield on the school trip before that, because he'd seen a plane he needed to investigate?

That certainly wasn't his fault — it was the school's, for not showing them anything interesting.

"Gondola ride on the Baby Bayou next, everyone," smiled *Miss Lovely*.

"*Yay*," trilled the infants.

"The gondolas are *so exciting*," said Goody-Goody Gordon.

"I don't want to go on the stupid gondola ride!" yelled Horrid Henry. "I want to go on the **ZOOM OF DOOM!!**"

"That's much too scary," said Perfect Peter.

"It's a straight drop to the bottom," GASPED Tidy Ted.

"I'm scared of heights," whimpered Perky Parveen.

"Don't worry, we won't be going anywhere near the **ZOOM OF DOOM**," said *Miss Lovely*.

"I want to go on the **ZOOM OF DOOM!**" howled Horrid Henry.

"Henry. Ralph. You're staying with me," said **MISS BATTLE-AXE.** "And that's final. There will be no repeat of last year. Or the year before that. And as I **DO NOT LIKE** water slides, we will be sticking with *Miss Lovely's* class."

"**NOOOOOOOOOOOO!**" howled Horrid Henry.

"**NOOOOOOOOOOOO!**" howled Rude Ralph.

"**YES**," snapped **MISS BATTLE-AXE**. She shuddered. **UGGHH.** She would rather swim with **SHARKS** than go on a water slide and be hurled backwards into an abyss. The very thought made her feel faint. Once when she was a little girl she'd tried a *teeny weeny* rollercoaster and spent a week recovering from the fright in

a darkened
room. No water
slides for her.

Horrid Henry scowled. He had
to escape from Miss Battle-Axe and
get on the **ZOOM OF DOOM**. He had
to. He loved **scary rides** and **BIG
DROPS** and **ROLLERCOASTERS** more
than **ANYTHING** in the whole wide
world. The *TWISTIER*, the **TURNIER**,
the more *terrifying* the better. And
— oh, the **AGONY** — here he was, finally,
at **WILD WATER-SLIDE PARK**, and he
was trapped with the infants.

He whispered to **RUDE RALPH**.

Ralph smiled.

"Good plan," he said.

Just as their giant teacup reached the dock, **RUDE RALPH** stood up, *wobbled* and *toppled* over the side into the river. He started **splashing** and **SHRIEKING.**

"Man overboard!" shouted Horrid

Henry. "**HELP! HELP!**" He'd escape in all the commotion and get straight on the **ZOOM OF DOOM** before anyone could stop him.

Henry leapt off the teacup.

A **hideous** hand grabbed his shoulder.

"Not so fast," said **MISS BATTLE-AXE.**

"Why aren't you rescuing Ralph?" screamed Henry. "He's drowning."

"**HELP!**" yelped Ralph, **SPLUTTERING** and **FLAILING**. "**HELP!**"

"Stand up, Ralph," said **MISS BATTLE-AXE**. "Now."

Slowly, **RUDE RALPH** stood up in the shallow water, which only reached his knees.

RATS.

"Everyone get in line and follow me to the Baby Bayou," trilled *Miss Lovely*.

"Yay," said Perfect Peter. "The Baby Bayou is my favourite ride."

Horrid Henry pinched Peter.

Perfect Peter screamed.

"Henry pinched me!" he wailed.

"I was just checking to see if you were an **alien**," *hissed* Henry. "And you are."

Moody Margaret and Sour Susan strolled past, laughing.

"Oh wow, that was so much fun," *squealed* Moody Margaret.

"Yeah," *squealed* Sour Susan.

"Let's go on the **ZOOM OF DOOM** now," said Margaret loudly. "And then **Belly Flop Drop** again."

"Yeah," said Sour Susan.

"Did you enjoy the giant teacups, Henry? I hope you weren't too scared," said Moody Margaret, smirking.

Horrid Henry gritted his teeth.

What could he say? Or do? Other than hope that a **GIANT SEA MONSTER** would rise up from the Lazy River and swallow Margaret whole.

"Too bad you won't get to ride the **ZOOM OF DOOM**, Henry," said Margaret.

"**NAH NAH NE NAH NAH**," jeered Margaret and Susan, racing off to join the long queue snaking away from the entrance to the **ZOOM OF DOOM**.

"We've got to escape," muttered Horrid Henry.

"Too right," said **RUDE RALPH**.

Henry looked at Ralph.

Ralph looked at Henry.

"Run!" shouted **Horrid Henry**.

Henry and Ralph ran off as fast as they could. They darted through the crowds, *pushing* and **shoving** and LEAPING, closer and closer to the ZOOM OF D—

CRASH! BANG!

"And where do you think you're going?" came a TERRIBLE voice.

Huh?

There was **MISS BATTLE-AXE** standing in front of them, arms crossed. They'd slammed right into her.

"We needed the loo," said Henry.

"It was an emergency," said RUDE RALPH.

MISS BATTLE-AXE glared at them.

"If you so much as move an INCH from my side again, you will be taken straight to the BAD CHILDREN'S ROOM to wait for your parents to collect you," said Miss Battle-Axe.

Yikes.

THE BAD CHILDREN'S ROOM.

If Henry got sent home he'd have NO chance of ever getting on the ZOOM OF DOOM. His parents would never take him back to WILD

179

WATER-SLIDE PARK, that was for sure.

He'd have to grit his teeth and find another way.

Horrid Henry and Rude Ralph followed the infants to the gondolas on the Baby Bayou.

"I feel **SEASICK**," said **RUDE RALPH** suddenly. "Those teacups made me dizzy. I need to go to the First Aid room." He **belched** loudly, then **WINKED** at Henry.

"**ohhhh!** Yeah, me too," said Horrid Henry. He clutched his stomach. **"OWN. OWWWW.** You can just leave

us to recover there," he moaned. "We don't want to stop anyone having fun."

Miss Battle-Axe took **Horrid Henry** and **RUDE RALPH**, groaning and moaning, to the First Aid room.

They lay down on two cots.

"No need to stay with us," **GROANED** Henry.

"We'll just lie here till it's home time," **MOANED** Ralph.

"These boys are suffering from seasickness," said **MISS BATTLE-AXE** to the nurse.

"Tummy ache?" said the nurse.

"Yes," moaned Henry.

"Dizzy?"

"Oh yes," said Ralph.

"Feeling like you are going to vomit?"

"Any second," said Henry.

"Not to worry," said the nurse.

"I have just the right injection." She advanced towards them, waving two 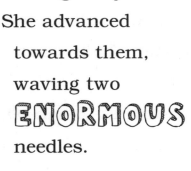 **ENORMOUS** needles.

"You know, I feel a lot better," said Henry, sitting up.

"Me too," said Ralph.

"Excellent," said **MISS BATTLE-AXE**. "Now off we go to the **Dozy Dinghies**. If we're lucky, we'll catch *Miss Lovely* at the steamboats for a relaxing journey around the *Pixie Pond*."

How was it possible, thought Henry miserably, trudging after her, to have so many baby rides in a water-slide park?

He could see Tough Toby and Fiery Fiona whizzing down **PANIC PRECIPICE**, whooping and laughing while he was trapped on the *Pixie Pond*.

"Last ride before home time," said *Miss Lovely*. "*Lullaby Lagoon* or the *Fairy Float Boats*?"

"*Lullaby Lagoon* might be too scary," said Spotless Sam.

"How about the **CANNIBAL CANOES,** where you get eaten as you ride?" snarled **Horrid Henry.** "That's why all the canoes come back empty."

"Quiet, Henry," said **MISS BATTLE-AXE.** Soon, she'd be safely home, with her feet up, and the school outing would

be over for another year.

"*Fairy Floats, Fairy Floats*," chanted the infants.

"Where are the *Fairy Float Boats*?" said *Miss Lovely*. Miss Battle-Axe consulted her map.

"Right next to the **ZOOM OF DOOM**," said **MISS BATTLE-AXE**, pointing to the huge queues jostling each other waiting for both rides.

Just to torture him, thought **Horrid Henry** as he plodded over to the queue for the *Fairy Float Boats*. Could his day have got even worse?

So near, and yet so far.

There were so many people *pushing* and **SHOVING** that the queues were starting to mix. You couldn't tell which queue was which.

And then Horrid Henry had a brilliant, **SPECTACULAR** idea. It was **perilous.** It was **DANGEROUS.** The chance of success was tiny. And yet . . . and yet . . . how could he not risk his life for a chance to ride the **ZOOM OF DOOM**?

"Come on, everyone, this way, this way," said Henry, weaving through

the **MASSIVE** queues. Perfect Peter, Goody-Goody Gordon and Tidy Ted followed him.

Slowly, Henry *inched* his way to the right into the **ZOOM OF DOOM** queue.

"Follow me," shouted **RUDE RALPH**, ushering **MISS BATTLE-AXE**, *Miss Lovely* and her class to the right behind Henry.

Finally they reached the head of the queue.

"What's this ride again?" asked Perky Parveen.

"*Fairy Float Boats*," said Henry,

grabbing a seat at the front of the **BLACK SKULL** raft.

"Oh, I love the Fairy Float Boats," said Perfect Peter.

Miss Lovely and **MISS BATTLE-AXE** sat down.

"I don't remember seat belts on the Fairy Float Boats," said Miss Battle-Axe, buckling up. "Do you, Lydia?"

"No," said Miss Lovely. "Must be new HEALTH AND SAFETY rules. Seat belts on, everyone."

The rubber rafts began a slow ascent up the track.

"Lydia," said Miss Battle-Axe. "I don't remember riding in **BLACK SKULLS** on the *Fairy Float Boats*, do you?"

"Must be a new design," said Miss Lovely.

The rafts climbed higher. Soft music began to play.

"Boudicca," said *Miss Lovely*, "don't we seem rather high up for the *Fairy Float Boats* . . ."

"Now that you mention it," said Miss Battle-Axe. She peered over the edge. "Lydia, I've got the feeling we're not—"

But before she could finish speaking

the raft PLUNGED over the edge, SPUN
BACKWARDS and PLUMMETED straight down.
MISS BATTLE-AXE screamed.

"AAAAARRRGGGGHHHIIE"

Miss Lovely screamed.

The infants screamed.

"WHOOPEEEEE!"
shrieked Henry and Ralph.
They'd done it. They were
riding on the ZOOM OF DOOM
at last.

Life was sweet.

Read on for some great games and puzzles!

Crossword

SOLVE THE CLUES AND FIT THE ANSWERS INTO THE GRID.

ACROSS

1. HENRY _ _ _ _ _ _ OVER THE OBSTACLES IN THE OBSTACLE RACE (6)

4. HENRY AND MARGARET HAVE TO RUN THE _ _ _ _ _ _–LEGGED RACE TOGETHER (5)

5. THE TUG–OF–WAR ENDS WITH ONE TEAM IN A MUDDY _ _ _ _ _ _ (6)

6. PETER IS IN CHARGE OF BRINGING THE HARD–BOILED _ _ _ _ TO SPORTS DAY (4)

DOWN

2. THE ONLY SNACK MISS BATTLE-AXE ALLOWS ON SPORTS DAY IS A PIECE OF _ _ _ _ _ _ (6)

3. AEROBIC AL HOPES TO WIN LOTS OF _ _ _ _ _ _ _ _ (8)

Musical Maze

CAN YOU HELP HENRY FIND HIS WAY THROUGH
THE MAZE TO GRAB THE KILLER BOY RATS
CONCERT TICKETS?

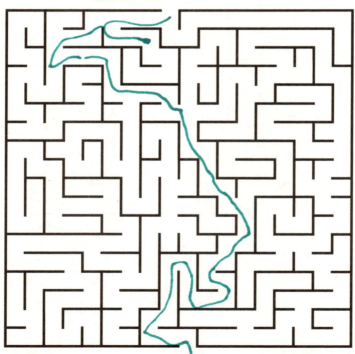

Wordsearch

CAN YOU FIND ALL THESE WORDS TO DO
WITH THE SCHOOL FAIR?

D	S	S	T	Y	G	B	M	U	J
O	U	B	R	S	U	M	M	E	R
L	P	R	E	S	U	P	P	E	A
L	E	O	A	C	I	H	R	S	R
N	R	O	S	U	S	L	O	D	Y
P	S	L	U	C	K	Y	D	I	P
I	O	C	R	I	A	B	A	N	R
B	A	K	E	R	R	O	N	G	I
C	K	I	M	N	T	U	C	O	Z
A	E	R	A	F	F	L	E	C	E
N	R	I	P	J	U	M	B	L	E

TREASURE MAP   RAFFLE   DANCE

LUCKY DIP   PRIZE   SUMMER

DOLL   SUPER SOAKER   JUMBLE

Spot the Difference

CAN YOU FIND SIX DIFFERENCES BETWEEN THESE PICTURES?

1 ☑   2 ☑   3 ☑

4 ☐   5 ☐   6 ☐

Jokes

HERE ARE SOME FUNNY SUMMER JOKES TO TELL YOUR FRIENDS!

How can you tell the sea is friendly?
Because it waves.

What do you call a snowman in
the summer? A puddle.

What do you get if you cross a fish
with an elephant? Swimming trunks.

What do ghosts eat in the summer?
Ice scream.

What's the best day to go to the beach?
SUNday.

What do you call a poodle in the summer?
A hot dog.

Word Scrambles

SOMEONE HAS SCRAMBLED THE TITLES OF
SOME STORIES FROM THIS BOOK!
CAN YOU WORK OUT WHICH IS WHICH?

STAYS DROP

FOOLISH CAR

MIMING SLOWNESS

SORT RACK

ROCK STAR

SCHOOL FAIR

SPORTS DAY

SWIMMING LESSON

Picture
Scavenger Hunt

LOOK BACK THROUGH THE BOOK AND
SEE IF YOU CAN FIND ALL THESE PICTURES . . .

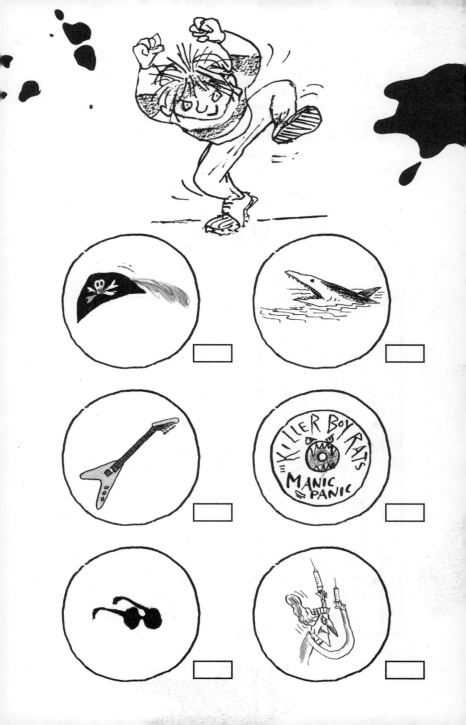

Maze of Doom

CAN YOU HELP HENRY AND RALPH FIND THEIR WAY
THROUGH THE MAZE TO GET TO THE ZOOM OF DOOM
BEFORE MISS BATTLE-AXE STOPS THEM?

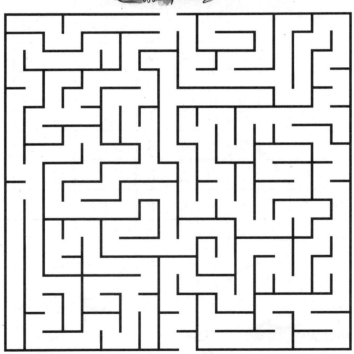

Woeful Wedding Wordsearch

CAN YOU FIND ALL THE WEDDING-RELATED WORDS IN THIS GRID?

P	C	U	M	M	E	R	B	U	N	D
B	H	C	G	R	A	P	S	E	N	T
R	C	O	R	A	L	M	I	N	D	B
I	R	N	T	O	P	H	A	T	O	R
P	I	F	G	O	B	I	L	L	A	I
E	N	E	K	W	G	R	O	O	M	D
T	G	T	B	O	Y	R	I	N	M	E
A	S	T	E	V	C	P	A	R	T	Y
L	R	I	N	G	S	A	M	P	E	L
S	F	O	R	D	L	L	K	I	H	E
A	P	A	G	E	B	O	Y	E	G	S

CUMMERBUND   BRIDE   CAKE

PAGEBOY   GROOM   PARTY

CONFETTI   RINGS   PHOTOGRAPHS

TOP HAT   PETALS

ANSWERS

Crossword

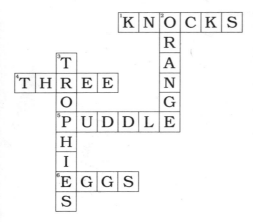

Musical Maze

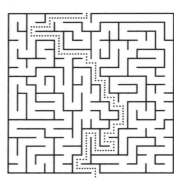

Spot the Difference

Wordsearch

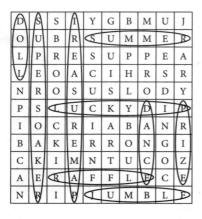

Word Scrambles

STAYS DROP ⟶ SPORTS DAY   MIMING SLOWNESS ⟶ SWIMMING LESSON

FOOLISH CAR ⟶ SCHOOL FAIR   SORT RACK ⟶ ROCK STAR

Picture Scavenger Hunt

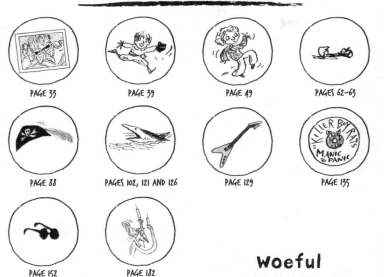

PAGE 33   PAGE 39   PAGE 49   PAGES 62–63

PAGE 88   PAGES 102, 121 AND 126   PAGE 129   PAGE 135

PAGE 152   PAGE 182

Maze of Doom

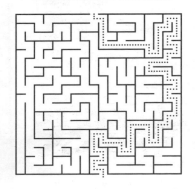

Woeful Wedding Wordsearch

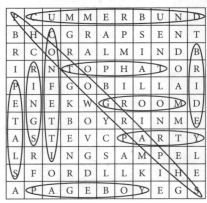

COLLECT ALL THE
HORRID HENRY STORYBOOKS!